Vinnie and Me

Prose Series 31

Fiorella De Luca Calce

Vinnie and Me

Guernica
Toronto / New York
1996

Antonio D'Alfonso, Editor
Guernica Editions Inc.
P.O. Box 117, Station P, Toronto (On), Canada M5S 2S6
340 Nagel Drive, Cheektowaga, N.Y. 14225-2802 U.S.A.

Legal Deposit — First Quarter
National Library of Canada

Library of Congress Catalog Card Number: 93-80984

Canadian Cataloguing in Publication Data
De Luca Calce, Fiorella, 1963 -
Vinnie and me
(Prose series ; 31)
ISBN 1-55071-017-6
I. Title. II. Series.
PS8557.E443V46   1994   C813'.54 C94-900057-4
PR9199.3.D44V46   1994

96 97 98 99 10 9 8 7 6 5 4 3 2 1

To My Best Friend C. P.

1

The muffled sound of the ball bouncing off the back-yard wall follows me into the house.

'Hey, Sis. You wanna throw a few.' My brother's voice cuts through the back-door windscreen.

'Maybe later,' I answer, dropping my grocery bags on the cluttered kitchen counter. I take a pan from the cupboard, fill it with water, sprinkle a bit of salt and set it on the stove.

'Come on, Piera.' My brother pokes his flushed face through the open window above the sink.

'I'm busy, Bennie.'

He wipes his forehead with the back of his hand. 'Phew! Hot. What's for supper?'

'Pasta.'

'Again.'

'Supper will be ready in fifteen minutes. How about setting the table?'

He groans, ducks his head back out. I put away the remaining groceries I picked up after school. The garden flowers on the table smell nice. Father probably won't notice. The door to his bedroom is open. I find him sprawled on the bed, his arm flung across his forehead, as if afraid someone would wake him up. His belt buckle is open, his feet bare.

'Papa.' I touch his shoulder. 'You can come and eat now.' I say in Italian.

His arm slides off his face, his eyes, sky blue, open, like Bennie's.

'*Piera, sei tu.* It's you.' He grunts, turns his head to the wall where a picture of my mother hangs above the bed. She died three years ago.

'Mr Tucci called this morning. I told him your ulcer was bothering you. He said it costs him every time you're sick. He wasn't too happy.' I pause. 'You need that job, Papa. We need to keep the house.'

He looks at me now, says in Italian: 'Just like your mother. You are just like your mother.' That familiar helpless look crosses his unshaven face. He pushes himself off the bed. I help him with his robe.

'Go ahead,' I tell him. 'I'll make the bed.'

He leaves the room; I change the bed sheets. My foot hits something cold: an empty bottle of wine. I kick it under the bed, turn out the light.

8:00 p.m. I still have not started my English project, been painting instead. The ocean, from an old greeting card someone gave me. I'd like to be able to paint a real one someday,

8

watch it on gentle days as it breathes against the shore or better still when it is restless, angry, violent; to be able to tame the waves and hold them still on a piece of canvas.

I stare at the journal lying next to me on my dresser drawer. The name Vinnie is scrawled on the blank page. I'm supposed to write in it for the remainder of the year. The first entry is supposed to describe the person closest to me. This happens to be Vinnie Andretti, my best friend. He is not an easy topic to tackle. No more than it is to finish this painting.

Tonight I started reworking the canvas, but the paint brush feels heavy, my strokes as uncertain as the words I had started to write in my journal. How can I write about Vinnie? How can I describe him when his character is as elusive as the moods that often cross his face? In third grade he dared me to sneak into old man Capelli's backyard with him, see who would eat the most apples. I won but we both got sick. We've been friends ever since. Vinnie says the reason we are such great friends is because we keep things in perspective. I prevent him from going too crazy; he, from my getting too serious.

What I like about him is that, in the evening, I can tell him to go fly a kite and that we would still be friends in the morning. According to my sister Gina, we are a weird couple: the Beauty and the Brain: I, the Brain; Vinnie, the Beauty.

Gina is married, lives on the South Shore of Montreal. She is pregnant, expects the baby for the Summer. She has become very maternal during the last couple of months.

My sister has her reservations about Vinnie. She thinks he is irresponsible, a little on the wild side, a bad influence. Deep down, I know she likes him. I guess he reminds her of herself at that age.

Gina is right, though; Vinnie is a little wild, careless. He makes an art of shocking people. As the time he pulled a mooner in front of Mrs B.. He wanted to show her his beauty mark.

He has a temper too. Last Christmas he smashed the display case in the Student Lounge because the monitor would not take his pass. If I had to name all the things that Vinnie likes, I could sum it up in these words: running laps around the neighbourhood track, travelling (though he has never really gone anywhere) and, I guess, hanging out with me. If it isn't for Vinnie, I probably would get through High School unnoticed. Girls are wild about him.

This is the last year of high school. Our last summer. We're supposed to take the summer off from our part-time job at MacDonalds and drive across Canada to B.C. We have had this trip planned since we were twelve. His grandfather had a stroke a year and a half ago and had to be put in a nursing home. He used to be in the landscape business and passed his truck on to Vinnie.

Vinnie does not think about such things as whether or not the truck will last the trip, or if we will have our part-time jobs to come back to. He just gets up and goes. All action, no talk.

Up until a month ago I would accompany Vinnie to the nursing home, but since Mr Andretti, his grandfather, got worse and they had moved him to the local hospital, now only family can visit him. So Vinnie goes without me. He likes to read the Italian newspaper to his grandfather. They are close to one another. For as long as I can remember, it was Mr Andretti who would greet us at the door after school. His face, always serious and polite. A man of few words, he would fix us a snack and allow us to putter around in his garden. Vinnie's mother was not around very much, still isn't. I never met Vinnie's natural father. All I know is he left before Vinnie was born.

Vinnie and his mother are like oil and water. She has a lot of male companions. They often crash out at the house, sometimes for weeks at a time. This drives Vinnie crazy. He says she does not know how to pick her friends.

I have seen a few characters come and go in that house. The worst was Max. I stayed away when Max was around. Didn't like the way he looked at me. As though I had nothing on. Vinnie caught him taking money from his mother's purse once. He tried to tell her. She called him a liar. Another time Vinnie found dope a friend of hers had stashed away in the basement. Vinnie flushed everything down the toilet.

Things really got out of hand. Vinnie would have killed the guy had Mrs Andretti not called the police. She said Vinnie was trying to drive her friends away. That hurt him; he never forgot it.

I admit, Vinnie gets a little crazy sometimes. Sometimes he says things that amaze me. I'm not supposed to say this but sometimes he wishes he were a woman, but only for a minute. He says he'd like to know what it feels like to be pregnant, to have something living inside him. What can I say about a guy like that. That's Vinnie.

These are the things I would like to write about but I do not think that Vinnie would appreciate that very much. Maybe I will write about his pick-up truck, about the garden we planted in my backyard, about his grandfather....

It's 9:00 p.m. Don't feel like sleeping yet. I leave the room, go into the kitchen, and pick up the phone.

'Yeah.' It's a man's voice.

'Can I talk to Vinnie, please?'

'Who's looking for him?'

'Piera.'

'He ain't here.'

'When do you expect him back?'

'How the hell should I know? You think I live here?'

I can hear Mrs Andretti's voice — 'Max, who is it?'— and the sound of the phone changing hands. 'Hello.'

'Mrs Andretti, it's Piera.'

'Vinnie isn't home, honey.'

'Do you know when he'll be back?'

'Damn kid never tells me anything. I'll have him call you when he gets in.'

I tell her not to bother; she hangs up.

I put on my windbreaker, check in on my brother (he is sound asleep), I slip out the front door.

The race track is two streets down from my block on Everett Street. I spot Vinnie amidst the poplar trees that surround the track and head over to the bleachers. He sees me, waves. He runs the track two more times then joins me. Strands of damp hair cling like seaweed to his face.

'You need a haircut.' I brush his bangs from his forehead. His face is cold.

'Yeah.' He expels his breath. 'What's up?'

'You want to go to my sister's on Sunday?'

'Sure, why not.'

'I called your house. You didn't tell me Max was back.'

13

'What for?' he shrugs, absently stroking his cheek. 'He will be gone after pay day.'

'I thought she kicked him out.'

'Some drug habits are hard to break.' He opens his hand. I hand him the towel crumpled next to me.

'What will you do?'

'It's her place. She can do whatever she wants.' He dries his face, wraps the towel around his neck.

'Where will you sleep tonight?' I ask him. He will not sleep at home because Max is there.

'Don't know.'

'You can stay at our house.'

'No.'

I sigh, wondering why I always bother with the question when I know the answer will be no.

'You can't camp out in the truck!' I reason.

He shrugs. 'What are you doing here anyway?'

'Couldn't sleep.'

'Something bothering you?'

'I have a French oral tomorrow. I didn't study this weekend.'

'You always do great,' he pats my shoulder.

I stare at the floor, shuffle my feet.

'Your dad is drinking again.' He holds my chin, catches my eyes, knowing I won't answer. I look away.

'Your dad needs the bottle like my mother needs men.'

'I hate it when you say things like that.'

He takes my arm, makes me look at him: 'You hate the truth.' The words hurt. He knows it. He pulls me to him, kisses my left temple. A smile escapes me. 'Come on, Perri. I'll walk you home.'

2

The school counsellor wants to see me today. There are two other students waiting on the couch. The one with orange hair has his face in a comic book, the other is busy cleaning his nails with a toothpick.

'Can I help you?' the secretary eyes me under thick eyelashes, her hair as neat as the top of her desk.

'I'm here to see Mr Jennings.'

'Do you have a note?'

I hand it to her. She takes it, disappears behind grey glass doors, and returns a few minutes later.

'You can go in.'

I head in the direction she came from. Mr Jennings beacons me from his office. 'Close the door.' He goes round his desk, pulls out a chair for me.

'You wanted to see me?' I ask.

He places his elbows on his desk, his hands cross. 'How are you keeping up in class?'

'Good.'

'At home?'

'Fine.'

He watches me, eyes levelled, pulls a file from his desk basket. 'You've had quite a few absences this semester.'

'My brother has been sick.'

'I assume you're still working weekends? And tutor after class?'

I nod, catch a glance at the students' marks hanging over his head. I had never seen them before.

He points his finger at me. 'You are doing too much.'

'I work hard.'

'I know. Your grades are excellent. You have been chosen class valedictorian. The Liddiard scholarship is as good as yours. That is quite a record, young lady. But,' he pauses, 'if you persist in taking on more than you can handle, you won't get through the term.' He waits for me to say something, pushes himself back in his chair when I don't. 'I see you finally decided on a college. Canadian Pacific has a good business program. As I recall, your aptitude test indicated the Arts.'

'It was the most sensible choice.'

'I noticed your friend, Vinnie Andretti, applied there too. Have either of you had a reply?'

'We waited until the last minute to make a decision.' I remember clearly because Vinnie delivered the applications in person so we wouldn't miss the deadline.

'You should have received a confirmation by now.'

He glances at his watch. 'It's almost noon.' His smile is reassuring. 'Let me look into it. See what the hold-up is in the Admissions Office.'

I get up, try not to appear too eager, breathe easier outside the office. I stop at my locker on the way to the cafeteria. Vinnie is sitting in the usual seat by the vending machines. I cut through the tables. Someone grabs my waist from behind.

'Hey professor.'

It's Sam Lopez, the student I have been tutoring. He's managed to sit me on his lap. 'Guess what?' he is grinning from ear to ear.

'What?' I try to sit up. I can feel Vinnie watching us.

'I got 90% on the French paper.'

His smile makes my stomach waltz.

'That's great, Sam. I knew you could do it.'

'Thanks to you. Those lessons we worked on really helped. Let me buy you lunch.'

'I can't. I'm meeting someone.'

'I'll see you tonight then.' He kisses my cheek, sends me off with a pat on my backside.

Vinnie follows me with his eyes as I sit down in front of him. His hands are folded across his chest. 'What's with him?'

'He passed his French paper.'

'With a tutor like you, how could he go wrong? Now you know why I hang around you.

A girl who is smart and not bad to look at. Sam is not stupid.'

'Sam worked hard all semester,' I point out.

'Don't give me that look.' He jabs his hand in my face.

'What do you mean?'

He leans forward. 'You don't think I can work hard.'

'You don't.'

'If I did. Could I kiss you too?'

It hits me. 'You're jealous!'

'He's in my photography class, doesn't mean I have to like him. I know his type. Sam is taking you for a ride.'

'You don't know him.'

'I'm from the same breed, Perri. He doesn't care about you. You'll get hurt.' He sits back in his seat with that satisfied look on his face that says he is completely right.

I feel a headache coming on. 'Vinnie, we have one hour for lunch. Let's not waste it arguing.'

He studies me, studies my sandwich. 'Wanna trade my tuna for your peanut butter?'

My friend, Francine, gives me a good-luck sign as she passes my desk. It is my turn to go up in front of the class. My eyes wander over the notes she left on the desk. I try to pick up where she left off, fumble with the papers. Monsieur Dallaire has this pained look on his

19

face. Why can't I remember a thing? Francine makes a sign at me. I guess I will have to fake it.

My mouth opens, the words tumble out. I must be saying the right thing because Monsieur Dallaire nods every once in a while. And then somewhere in the building an alarm goes off, drowning out my words. Arms and legs scramble out of their seats. My teacher is already making his way towards me. I move from the blackboard. He stops me with his hand.

'*A demain, mademoiselle D'Angelo?*'

'*Oui...*, Sir.' I mumble, eager to follow the flow of students outside.

Francine moves up behind me, grabs my arm. 'Isn't this a first. Miss Perfect, Miss Brain is actually unprepared for an oral. What have you and Sam been working on besides the French project this weekend?'

'I didn't see him this weekend.'

Francine has what she calls a 'mega-crush' on Sam. Then, again, Francine has tons of crushes.

'You get Super Hunk for a partner, and who does Miss Bruillet stick me with? Dirtbag Sansalone.'

She means Pat Sansalone. He is the one guy in high school who does not understand the word *deodorant*.

'I spent the weekend helping Vinnie with his Math.'

'You know I couldn't believe it when he told me he applied to study in a cegep.'

'He has to do something.'

'I can't figure you two out. How come you're not going together?'

'Me and Vinnie?' The idea makes me laugh. 'We've known each other since fourth grade. He's almost my brother.'

'Not to mention blonde, adorable, and funny. How many girls can say that about their best friend.'

Francine elbows the guy in back of us as we go through the front entrance. 'Hey! Quit pushing, will you!'

That is the kind of thing I like about her.

Our principal, Mr Malone, is pacing the parking lot. Half the school is outside: the seniors on the right, the juniors on the left.

'Speaking of the devil.' Francine has spotted Vinnie in the parking lot.

He is leaning on the fender of a red Honda. He sees us, smiles, and strides towards us.

'So what do you girls think?' He winks at us. 'Perfect timing, huh?'

'You're responsible for this?' Francine gapes at him.

'What if you got caught.' I try not to raise my voice.

'What a guy!' Francine swings her arms around him. He rolls his eyes at me, pulls her closer.

'You are crazy.' I say under my breath.

'Only about you,' he lets go of her.

Francine gives me a what-did-I-tell-you look, then scans the crowd. 'Umm.... I think I see something I like.' She waves at a black-haired guy near the fence.

'My date for Saturday.' She winks. 'Catch you later.'

Her long hair whips my face, as she cuts after him. The alarm has stopped ringing. Vinnie takes my books. He follows me inside the school.

'You're quiet. Are you mad?'

'You tell me.' I stop walking.

'What have I done?' He throws up his hands.

I elbow him, nod towards the end of the corridor. Mr Malone is heading our way. He stops, gives Vinnie a hard, long stare.

'Andretti, how many detentions have you had this month?'

'I lost track.' Vinnie's face is square. God, don't let him argue.

'Well, Andretti, I haven't. If I didn't know better I would say you were responsible for this.'

'No, Sir.' I step in. 'He's been with me.'

The principal looks at me, then at Vinnie. 'The both of you get to class.'

I tell Vinnie to move. 'Five detentions. Four fights. No wonder they kicked you off the track team.' I hiss as soon as we lose sight of the principal.

'So I have a temper.' Vinnie shrugs.

'Last week you blew up the chemistry lab.'

'A miscalculation.'

'Friday you sent Mrs Goldstein to the nurse.'

'She was having a bad day.'

'Vinnie, you are every teacher's bad day. Sometimes I think you have no intention of graduating.'

'Are you kidding! One more year of this dump and I would go crazy. After the finals I'm out of here.'

'That might be sooner than you think. Mr Malone has you on his black list. One more stunt, and you're out. You know what that would do to your college application?'

'As if I have a hope in hell of getting in. I don't know why I applied there anyway,' he says wryly.

'You can't be a bum all your life. Besides, you can do it. I know you can do it.'

'So you're not mad at me?' His lips turn up at the sides in a Garfield smile.

'How can I? You're my ride home.'

3

It is different when I am at Sam's house. An only child, his parents adore him. His father is a CEO in the federal government; his mother is a school-teacher. They are very nice people, sophisticated, but down to earth.

For supper tonight Mrs Lopez served a dish with a name I can't remember. She always makes fancy dishes, and sometimes we have imported wine with our meal. She always makes dessert. Tonight it is *mille feuilles*, my favourite.

'It's wonderful how well Sam is doing now that he's agreed to peer tutoring. You've done wonders with him.' Mrs Lopez beams at me, her long black hair framing her olive-skinned face. Sam is more like his father, straight-haired and square-faced.

'I understand you'll be going to Canadian Pacific as well,' Mr Lopez directs the sentence at me.

'Yes. In the Business program, if all goes well, of course.'

'The girl is a brain.' Sam rubs my shoulder possessively.

'Sam will be working for my stockbroker this summer,' Mr Lopez says.

'Mail runs mostly,' Sam explains.

'Come to think of it,' Mr Lopez taps the table with his fingers, 'they might be able to use extra help in the secretarial pool. Do you type, Piera?'

'I took a typing course last semester.'

'That's great,' He pats my hand. 'The office might need some extra help. It would be good experience for you. A good job is hard to find nowadays.'

'Tell me about it,' Sam agrees. 'It beats working at MacDonalds.'

I wince at his words, glad I did not tell him I work there.

'Mom, Dad, did you know Piera is an artist,' Sam announces.

'It's good to have a hobby,' Mr Lopez says, as his wife refills his glass.

'Paint or pencil?' Mr Lopez asks.

'Both.'

"Say!' Sam snaps his fingers, 'aren't you participating in the Art Exhibit this year? Vinnie says your work is one of the school's best.'

'I doubt it. I haven't been painting much.'

'Did you know Vinnie is in my photography class?'

'Yes.'

'He takes good pictures.'

'I wouldn't know.' I shrug, counting the number of times he asked me to pose only to be told later that the pictures had not come out. 'He's been taking pictures as long as I've known him, but he never shows me any of them.'

'Is Vinnie a friend of your's?' Mr Lopez asks me.

'My best friend.'

Mr Lopez nods, then changes the topic to the evening's news. After supper I help Mrs Lopez with the dishes while the men play pool in the den. Once the chores are done, I gather my things, thank Mrs Lopez for supper, then wait for Sam to join me in the living room.

'Vinnie is picking you up tonight?' Sam comes in, a sour look on his face.

'Your dad beat you again?' I nod, while keeping an eye on the window for headlights.

'Why won't you let me drive you home?'

'Vinnie doesn't mind.' I did not want to explain that Vinnie and I always get together after supper. We either go for a walk, hang out at the track, or just sit on my front porch. It's like an old habit.

'I'm jealous.'

His honesty takes me off guard.

A horn honks outside.

'It's him.' I grab my bag, get up from the couch.

'Wait.' Sam pulls me back as I open the front door. He takes my face between his hands, kisses me on the lips.

'Goodnight,' I stammer, then stumble out into the street.

4

This morning, inside the living room, I find my brother sprawled on the couch with his head buried in a textbook. I peer over him.

'Homework? Hum?' I snatch the comic book he has hidden between the pages of his book.

'Aw, come on, Perri!' he swings at me.

'If you are going to lie down on the sofa, the least you could do is take off your shoes.' I pull his feet off the couch and place the bowl of soup on the coffee table.

'I'm sick.' My brother gives me a wounded look, folds his book on his head. 'Why can't Pop stay home instead of you?'

'Because Pop brings in the money,' I say, then stop to listen to the clattering sounds coming from the kitchen. Vinnie is in there making himself a sandwich.

'Next time you'll think twice about eating a jar of peanut butter. I have to miss a day of school because of you.'

Vinnie steps into the living room, his mouth full. 'Give the kid a break.'

'Shouldn't you be in school this morning,' I snap at him.

'School isn't fun without you. Besides you would miss me.' He shoves the sandwich in my face. 'Want some.'

I shake my head, bend to pick up this morning's newspaper from the floor. He grabs my waist and pulls me down on the sofa with him.

'Vinnie, cut it out. I've got things to do. I'm going upstairs for a while.' I punch him so that he will let me go. 'You think the two of you can stay out of trouble?'

They look at each other and grin. I hear a thud as I climb the stairs to my room — I hope they knock each other out. The dress I pulled out of my closet early this morning is on my bed. My room used to be my mother's sewing room. Her sewing machine sits in the far corner of the room. It's the only thing I kept of hers. I get to work, cut, baste, stitch the sides of the dress to fit my waist. Fifteen minutes elapse when I hear movement. I look up.

'Catch!'

My arm automatically reaches for the ceiling, my hand closes over the ball.

'I haven't got time.' I throw the ball back at Vinnie. He catches it and steps from the doorway into my room.

'Is that the dress you borrowed from Gina?'

'Umm.' I rest some pins between my lips.

'You should get a new one.'

'Can't afford one.'

I glance at the sandwich in his hand as he towers over me, watching me work.

'You're dropping breadcrumbs on my floor.'

'Sorry.'

'How can you eat so much and still be so skinny?' I drop the scissors.

'Metabolism.' He picks the scissors up, hands them to me, moves towards my bed. 'We will make a spiffy couple; you, in blue, and me, in black.' He lowers himself, scattering my stuffed animals. 'You know, that reminds me of the time we got all dressed up and crashed that wedding at Buffet Louis XV. Remember?'

'That was a long time ago.'

I check my watch. 'It must be recess. If you go back now no one will know you were missing.'

'Nice try.' He bounces off the bed, walks over to the canvas on my hope chest. He studies the painting.

'Have you decided what you want to display at this year's art exhibition.'

'I'm not participating.'

'Why not? You participate every year.'

'I haven't worked on anything new.'

'You've been working on Sam.' His glance is slanted, sarcastic.

He moves over to my bookcase, chooses a book and lowers himself on the bed.

'I like a girl that's cultivated.'

'Cultured.'

'That too.'

'Here.' I hand him the dress. 'Seeing that I'm stuck with you for the rest of the day, make yourself useful.'

A frown creases his brow.

'I have to hem it,' I explain.

'There is no way I'm getting into that thing,' his eyes widen, he gets off the bed.

I pull the dress over his head. He ducks, his arm snakes out, throwing me off balance. I fall over him, grab his leg so he can't get away. His head hits the floor, his eyes close.

'Seeing stars?' I touch his forehead.

His eyes open. 'No, an angel.'

The phone rings. He gets to it before I do.

'D'Angelo residence. You stab 'em, we slab 'em.'

I glare at him, make a knife cut at my throat, afraid it might be the school.

'It's Romeo.' He hands me the phone.

'Sam?'

Vinnie is making strangled sounds in back of me. I have trouble hearing him.

'...My brother is sick.... What...? ...Saturday...?' I look at Vinnie. 'Fine.' A sharp ring cuts through, signalling that recess is over.

'So,' Vinnie circles around me after I hang up. 'How is Romeo? Been hanging around you a lot lately.'

I pick up the dress from the floor.

'Sam is fine. You know what you need, Vinnie?'

'What?'

'A girlfriend.'

'I have a girlfriend.' He pats my nose.

'You know what I mean.' I brush his hand away. 'Francine isn't the only girl that has her eye on you. I can think of a few others. The only reason they hang out with me is because of you.'

'My best friend happens to be a girl. What more does a guy need?'

'That doesn't ride too well with the girls.'

'They still think I'm charming.'

'You mean a flirt.'

'I'm fun.'

'You're silly.'

'Yeah, but how many guys do you know who would do this for you?' He raises his arms as I throw the dress over his head.

'That's why I hang out with you.'

5

Saturday night. My father stops me in the corridor as I make my way downstairs. He glances at the dress I am wearing, says: 'You look pretty.'

My heels click on the steps that lead to the living room. Vinnie and Bennie are sitting on the sofa. They look at me, at each other, then back at me.

'Woosh!' Vinnie whistles. 'You didn't have to dress up on my account.'

'I didn't.'

My mouth feels dry. I walk to the kitchen for a glass of water.

'She has a date.' I hear Bennie whisper.

No longer thirsty, I realize I am stalling. I catch my father make a sign at Bennie with his hand. My brother follows him. Vinnie and I are alone.

'So,' he pats the seat beside him. 'Romeo is your date tonight.'

I sit down next to him. He rests his hand on my shoulders, plays with the straps of my dress. I brush his fingers off. 'Sam is going to be here in a few minutes.'

He lifts his eyebrows.

I turn on the television set, can feel his eyes on me.

'You're wearing too much lipstick.'

'I like it this way.'

'...Where are you guys going?'

'To a movie.'

'You knew I wasn't working tonight. I thought we were going bowling or something, like usual.'

'Sam asked me out. I said *yes*.'

'Why didn't you tell me?'

The sound of the doorbell saves me from answering. In my haste to get up, my skirt gets caught in my heel. The dress does not tear.

'Sorry I'm late. Car trouble,' Sam says.

I let him in. He wipes his feet on the carpet, glances at Vinnie with a nod, steps on the wooden floor. He looks handsome in his cashmere sweater and tailored grey pants. I can feel Vinnie eyeing him up behind me.

'I'm ready. I just need a sweater,' I tell him.

'Here.' Vinnie gets up from the sofa, hands me the sweater lying next to him. His fingers clasp mine as I take it from him.

'You look beautiful.' He moves forward, brushes a kiss on my cheek. His eyes hold me, then turns to Sam as though seeing him for the first time.

'Make sure you buy her popcorn. She's crazy about the stuff.' He gives Sam a pat on the arm then walks out the front door.

'Did I miss something,' Sam raises his eyes at me.

'Give me a minute?' The words come out strangled.

He nods. I step outside, cross the street. Vinnie is sitting in his grandfather's truck. He pulls out a rag from the floor and starts wiping his rear-view mirror, ignoring me. I get in the truck, slam the door behind me.

'I'm sorry, I should have told you.'

He remains silent, continues wiping the mirror, then says: 'Do you like this guy?'

'I guess. Why?'

'Like what is it? You guys going steady?' He leans against the window on his side, as though he wants to leave as much distance between him and me.

'No.'

'Could have fooled me.'

'What difference does it make? What does it have to do with me and you?'

'Everything. Why didn't you tell me you were seeing him tonight?'

'Maybe because I knew you wouldn't like it.'

He turns towards me, shakes his head, bends over me to open the door, waits for me to get out. I step out, go stand in front of the window on his side, hoping he will say something. He doesn't. He guns the motor instead, leaves me standing there in the fumes of the exhaustion. My chest feels tight. I cross my

35

arms to stop the feeling. Sam comes up behind me, puts his hand on my shoulder. I had almost forgotten him.

'Everything okay?'

'Sure.'

He walks me to his car, opens the door. I feel suddenly different, expensive, as I slide into the front seat. He starts to drive around the block, then moves into a spot facing the race track. I turn to him. He slips his arm around me, pulls me close. He kisses me, draws away when I don't respond. 'Is something wrong?'

I sit back against the seat, stare at the dashboard.

'Perri, I like you. I thought you liked me too.'

'I do, but....'

'But what? You and Vinnie have something going?'

'Of course not!' I snap.

'Why do you hang around him anyway? What is a smart girl like you doing with a clown like him. Everyone knows he is a loser.'

'He is my friend. I've known him longer than I've known you.'

'I'm sorry.' His tone softens. 'That was mean of me.' He runs his hand up my arms, on my neck, draws me close again. I push against him.

'Don't be a tease,' he whispers now into my ear.

I immediately open the car door.

'Perri, wait!' He grabs my waist.

'Sam, all I had in mind was a movie.'

'Fine. Get in. Please.'

I hesitate.

'A movie it is. Promise.'

I get in. He starts the car.

The movie is long. Maybe it is because I have already seen it with Vinnie. The giant screen becomes a huge moving canvas on which my childhood is painted. Perri and Vinnie sitting in a tree, kissing. Our bellies full of apples. We run because the old man is yelling at us. Mamma is waiting for us. She scolds us because we are sick and she has to hold both our foreheads over the toilet bowl. But inside you know she is laughing. My father calls Vinnie's mother. She says he can sleep over. Later at night we prowl downstairs. My sister is sitting on the couch with her new boyfriend. I think Leo was his name. Gina and Leo sitting in a tree, kissing...

The movie is over. On the way home we stop for donuts and coffee. He later drives me home. I don't ask him in. He doesn't seem surprised.

The light is on in the kitchen. I find my father sitting at the table, reading a circular.

'Papa, you didn't have to wait up for me.'
I take off my sweater, drape it on the chair.

'Couldn't sleep. Damn stomach,' he says in Italian.

'Maybe some tea will help.'

I fill the kettle with water and put it on the stove.

'How was the movie?'

'*Bene.*'

'*Bello ragazzo, quello Sam*. He's going to college?'

'Yes.'

'I'm old but I can still notice things.... You and Vinnie.... *Cos'è successo?*'

I smile. 'You know us. We always fight. How else would we get along.'

'Are you still going to Gina's tomorrow?'

'Yes.' But with the way things were I wasn't sure.

'It's late.' He pushes the chair beside behind him, raises himself on his hands.

'You must be tired, Papa?'

'*Sì*. You should get to bed too.' He turns his back to me. He is across the living room when I stop him.

'Come with us, Pappa. It would make Gina happy.'

I know my words are useless. He is already up the stairs, pretending not to have heard me.

Once in my room, I take out my easel, prepare my paints. I look outside my window into the backyard. Sometimes I think I can see all of us sitting around the picnic table — when we were a real family, with Mamma and Gina.

I sketch quickly. A young girl sitting in front of a doorstep, her head bent, her arms cradling the swollen stomach. Her feet are bare, her toe-nails painted red. A broken doorknob rests on the cracked sidewalk. It is too late to start in the paint. Now I can sleep.

6

'I'll take those.' My sister takes the cups from my hands and places them back on the dish rack. 'They dry by themselves.'

'I don't mind. Besides, I would rather stay here and talk to you than watch football.' I turn my attention to the living room, Vinnie, Bennie and my brother-in-law, Paul, are huddled in front of the T.V.

'I can't wait for the baby to be born,' I pull out a chair from the table for her.

'Everything should go smoothly this time,' she huffs, lowering herself on the chair, legs spread apart. 'You can tell Father that I'm not about to lose this one.'

'Don't be hard on him, Gina. You really hurt him. You left home, moved in with a guy who wasn't Italian. You got pregnant and he dumped you. That was a heavy load to take. Especially for Mother. She kept hoping you would come back. Even after you lost the baby.'

'You can't go back to things, Piera.' She stares at an invisible spot on the wall, remembering. 'Does he ask about me sometimes?' She looks like a little girl again, small and unsure.

'He asked me when the baby was due. And if Paul was treating you right.'

'Why does he have to be so pig-headed and proud?' Her hand snatches the pack of cigarettes off the table, her fingers tug nervously at the wrapping.

'He says the same about you.' I take it from her, exchanging this comment for a piece of chewing gum taken from my pocket.

'Is he still drinking?'

I shrug, not wasting an answer.

Gina watches, absently wiping invisible crumbs from the table. 'You know, if you get accepted at the Art Institute, you would have to live on campus. It's too far for you to commute there everyday. We have a big house. Why don't you live with us? You would have your own room. There is an elementary school for Bennie and.... '

'Don't start this again, Gina. I'm not leaving him.' My stare cuts her words.

'Father isn't good for you.'

'That's what you said about Vinnie.'

'That's different. Father is going to kill himself one day.'

'He did a pretty good job raising us. Just because you screwed up doesn't mean you can blame it on him.'

Gina sits back in her chair, her face white.

41

One hand grips the table, the other her stomach.

My hands go to her waist. I cannot tell which one of us is paler. 'I'm sorry. I didn't mean it.'

'It kicked.' Her smile is strained.

'I didn't mean what I said.'

'Yes, you did. I've made mistakes, and I will pay for them. You can't save him, Perri. He is killing himself; it won't be long before one of you gets hurt.'

'I can't leave him.'

There is a knock.

'Don't mean to butt in....' Vinnie is standing awkwardly in the doorway. 'We're out of chips.'

'Top right shelf.' Gina motions with her head.

He goes to the cupboards, opens one, finds what he was looking for and exits without a backward glance.

'He doesn't seem himself,' Gina says when Vinnie is gone. 'Everything okay between you two?'

'Why do you ask?'

'You hardly spoke to each other during lunch. You're not still arguing about College?'

'We both want to go to Canadian Pacific.'

'Vinnie in College?' She shakes her head. 'It's like putting a tiger in a cage. He's too restless. What happened to your Art school?'

'Too expensive.'

'There is Mamma's money. Couldn't you use that?'

'I made my choice.'

'Obviously the wrong one.'

'You sound like Vinnie.'

'He knows a good thing when he sees it.'

'Deep down you really like him, don't you?'

'You think I would have him over for lunch if I didn't. Besides he gets you here in one piece,' she teases.

'I wasn't sure we would come today,' I admit.

'So you did argue.'

'Not really. Remember Sam?'

'Yes, the hispanic boy.'

'I've gone out with him a couple of times. Vinnie isn't happy about that. I don't see why. He still picks me up every morning. We go to school, I see him at recess and lunch. He waits for me beside his pick-up truck at the end of the day. He's always there. And when he isn't, I usually know where to find him. Nothing has changed.'

'Until now.' My sister smiles at me. Like she sees what is happening and understands it. 'Now there is this new guy. Maybe Vinnie feels that one day he won't need to wait for you, and maybe one day you might not need to know where to find him. Do you understand, Perri....'

My sister's words circle in my head. Vinnie hardly says a word to me all the way home. When we get to the house I tell Bennie to go in without me.

Vinnie stares absently through the windshield, then fiddles with the radio. I turn it off. I face him. 'What's happening to us?'

'I don't know,' he sighs, resting his head on the steering wheel. 'We used to talk. You used to tell me things. You've changed.'

'No, I haven't. Okay, so I've gone out with Sam once or twice.'

'I don't remember you ever dressing up for me. You're even starting to wear make-up. You never liked make-up. Heck, Perri, it's more than Sam,' he sighs. 'We used to talk about stuff, like going to Vancouver, about me fishing and you painting the ocean. Now all I hear is Canadian Pacific and Sam. I get the feeling you don't really want to go away this summer.'

'Would that be so bad. There is no reason why we couldn't stay in town and work through the summer, make some extra money.'

'See what I mean. You don't want to go anymore. Why didn't you tell me? We planned this trip since we were twelve. This is our last summer, Perri.'

'We were kids then; things are different now.'

'Yeah, real different. We used to do stuff, have fun. Remember that game we used to play. You would close your eyes and I would

44

try to guess what you saw. You would describe it for me, so I could see it too. Now you close your eyes and you see something I can't. You know what scares me the most?'

He closes his eyes.

'What?'

'I'm not sure I want to.'

I want to tell him to be quiet but instead I say.

'Vinnie, you don't have to go to college if you don't want to. But you have to think about the future. You have to do something.'

'I don't know what I want. I'm not smart like you.'

'That's a poor excuse.'

'What is your excuse? You give up painting for some boring office job.'

'I don't know about you but I'm not familiar with many rich artists. You think I will make money selling a couple of paintings on Ste. Catherine Street. My father will retire in a couple of years. The house has to be paid. Someone has to take care of Bennie.'

'You sound like a forty year old. You worry too much.'

'You don't worry at all. I want things, Vinnie.'

'You mean you want a guy like Sam. Let him drive you around in a fancy car. Wear nice clothes, probably end up working in some cushy office for some boring, bossy jerk who calls himself a professional.'

'No, I want a house that I can call my own. I want to wear clothes that aren't hand-me-downs. I want to be able to wear a real prom dress. Is that too much to ask for?'

'No, I guess not.'

'I hate worrying about money. Ever since I can remember we worried about money. My paintings won't pay the bills.'

'Maybe not. But I tell you. I've watched you paint. I've watched your face. You live in your colors. Your soul is in those paintings.'

I don't know what to answer him.

'Why do you have to be on top of everything? Why do you have to have everything figured out?' he goes on, shaking his head like he always does when I will not listen.

'What are you talking about?' I sigh.

'I can hear the words in that little head of yours. Don't leave any threads hanging, don't leave any space empty. What are you afraid of?'

'Since when did you become my shrink?'

'I don't remember us having so many differences. Do you?'

'No.' I rest my head against his shoulder.

He pulls me closer. 'You'll be a somebody some day.'

His words are almost a whisper, as if he's talking to me from some faraway place. I close my eyes, resting them a bit. When I open them again, something pulls within me. The stooped figure stumbling towards the house is my father.

46

'Where has he been?' Vinnie asks.

'Mario's Bar.'

'Come on.' He opens the car door. 'Let's get him inside.'

My father places his hands on our shoulders. He tries to steady himself as we help him up the porch.

'You kids had a good time?'

'Yes, Pappa.'

'So Vinnie, when are you gonna cut that hair of yours? You're beginning to look like a girl.'

'Don't tell me you're jealous Mr D'Angelo.'

'I wish I were your age again.' My father fumbles in his pocket for his keys. 'Don't be late coming in.'

'I guess I better be going too,' Vinnie says after my father shuts the door behind him. 'You'll be okay?' He rubs my shoulders.

I nod, rest my cheek on his hand. 'Thanks.'

'For what?'

'For being here.'

'Any time.'

'I'll see you in the morning.'

'You can count on it.'

7

Mr Jenning's stops me in the hallway on my way to class today. He looks disturbed. 'Would you come in my office, Piera?'

'Won't I be late for class?'

'The secretary will give you a note.' He insists, leaving me no choice but to follow him. We step into his office. He closes the door behind us. I notice he does not sit down, nor does he ask me to.

'I spoke to the coordinator of the Admissions department. They have no record of your applications.'

'That can't be. We filled them out late. Vinnie brought.... them... in... person.' Vinnie? Would Vinnie do that...? Suddenly I remember all the arguments, the coaxing.

The expression on Mr Jenning's face mirrors my own. His meaning is clear. 'There is someone you should be talking to,' he says gently.

All I want to do is get out of there. I must have mumbled something. Mr Jenning's does not try to stop me. The corridors are empty, endless. Their silence chases me out.

The paintbrush trembles in my hands as I cover the canvas with paint. Black and white and grey. I need to work on something new. The outline of a child sitting in dirt, clearing a garden full of weeds with an old paintbrush. His hands stab at the earth. An old man is sitting in a chair, eyes closed. I find myself darkening the faces, the garden, the sky, as if to erase everything. There is a knock at my door. I check my watch. I put down my paintbrush. My hand aches.

'Vinnie is here,' my father says.

'I don't want to see him.'

'Better if you did. Looks like he won the 6/49. Is that new?' He comes in, looks over my work.

'Yes.'

'I like it. It will look nice in the living room.'

'*Sì.*' I wipe my hands on a rag and follow my father downstairs. Vinnie is sitting on the front steps. He leaps to his feet when the door slams shut.

'Where were you? I waited for you until 4:30 p.m. Never mind. Here.' He digs in the pocket of his jacket. 'They came in the mail today.' He hands me some papers. It is a road map and a bunch of brochures of British Columbia. 'See, it's all figured out. I calculated the miles and everything. Even jotted down a few addresses of places were we can....' He searches my face. 'What's the matter?'

'Why, Vinnie?'

'Why what?'

'You never did hand in those applications did you?'

He backs away, leans his head on the porch railing.

'You know.'

'Yes.'

'How?'

'Mr Jenning's called the school. They never received them.'

'I was going to tell you.'

'When? Did you think I was never going to find out?'

'I did it for you.'

'You did it for yourself.'

'I can't see you chained to a desk, shuffling papers all your life. You were born to paint.'

'This isn't sixth grade, it isn't funny. That was my future you played with. You may not give a damn about yours but I do about mine. You think I want to end up like you.'

'What is that supposed to mean?' he says, red patches beginning to stain his face.

'You are not going anywhere. You don't give a damn about anything. Being cute and funny won't cut if forever you know. When are you going to grow up?' My words hurt him. I can see it on his face. 'Why didn't you tell me you didn't want to go to college?' I demand.

'I got through high school because of you. Your sister is right. I don't know what I want.

One thing's for sure, I do know what I don't want. I don't want college and to sell my dream or give up what I believe in.'

'You have no dream.' My laugh is bitter. 'You don't believe in anything.'

He steps away from me, his hands gripping the railing. I want to stop him. Can't. He is at the bottom. He turns around, faces me.

'I believed in you.'

8

Has it been weeks? Didn't think it would hurt this much, but it did. Seeing them together this morning, sitting so close beneath the tree. Francine waved at me. I faked a smile. Vinnie pulled her to him. They kissed. I hated him, had to turn away.

'Cute couple,' Sam had pulled me close, as if afraid I would disappear.

'Yes,' was all I could think of saying.

He made me look at him. 'Has a hell of an attitude though. Did you see that fight yesterday morning. He nearly ripped the guy's head off.'

'I know,' I mumble, remembering what the latter looked like. His lip cut, his nose bleeding. Vinnie had stared down at him in disgust, then he'd looked up and stared right at me. Didn't think he'd see me among the crowd but he had. And suddenly I felt as if the whole thing had been for me. All the anger and the hate had been for me. Someone standing next to me asked me what it was all about. I said I didn't know, didn't want to find out. So I ran, shutting my eyes, my heart...

Supper is silent tonight. My father watches me.

'Bennie, you know what I told you about reading at the table.' I hide my emotions beneath biting words.

'Let the boy be.' My father refills his glass with wine. 'He might be a lawyer someday.'

'That's right.' Bennie makes faces at me, turns to speak to my father. 'It's parents night at the end of the month.'

'You, in trouble?' My father's face darkens momentarily.

'No.'

My father looks at me. 'So why do I have to go?'

'Papa, it's obligatory,' I say.

'My English is no good.'

'I can't go this time, Papa. I have exams to study for,' I quickly make clear.

'What is wrong, Piera? Why the face?'

'She had a fight with Vinnie,' Bennie says promptly.

'Is that true? I don't see him anymore.'

'Yes.' I begin to clear the table.

'What happened?'

'Nothing.' I let the water run from the sink, hoping to drown out any questions.

'Piera stop washing. You can do the dishes later. I have something to tell you.'

I sit down. My father begins his usual litany. He rambles on about a truck, maybe going into the landscape business. I do not pay attention, because every month he comes up with some new idea we do not have the money for. Afterwards I go to my room and try to finish my ocean. The colours are perfect, the waves real. I feel them wash over me. I can't breath, my hands tremble as they work. When I look at the painting again. There are faint lines flowing up from the water to form one, no two... bodies... swallowing each other.

9

There is a good turnout this evening. The school was clever to hold the Art Exhibition in the cafeteria instead of the auditorium like last year. It has allowed them to display additional artwork. A few of my classmates and teachers came up to me, asking where my display was. I give them the well-rehearsed explanation. My art teacher says it is just as well, it will give someone else a chance to stand in the spotlight.

Sam has wandered off somewhere. I look for the rest rooms, hoping to avoid further questions. Francine is in there. I say 'Hi' to her. She mumbles her answer, acts as if the contents in her purse have suddenly become interesting. I go into a cubicle. When I come out, she is gone. She probably came with Vinnie.

Back in the cafeteria I scan the crowd for signs of Sam. I figure he is probably in the photography section. I walk by the table of sculptures, circle the panels of pictures, some black and white, some colour, and then I stop. The girl in the next picture stares back at me.

She is thirteen, trying on a dress that is twice her size as her mother smiles down at her, a thread and needle in hand. There is another. The same girl — holding a paintbrush in one hand and a pencil in the other. She is bent over the untouched canvas on her knee, as though she were able to see something I can't. In the others she is older, in one she sits on bleachers, elbows resting on her knees, hands cupping her face, bored. In another she is playing catch with her brother, her face flushed, eyes bright. There are others, capturing different moods, but it is the last one that tugs my insides. She is leaning against a brick wall. Looking off somewhere — looking for someone — waiting. All those pictures. He titled them *Best Friend*. All of them me. And not one of them did I pose for. He had taken them when I wasn't looking.

My eyes blur. I brush my eyes, not wanting anyone to see. When I take my hands away. I see him half-hidden behind a panel. His legs move to step back but my eyes hold him. This stranger, my best friend. It is only when I lower my gaze that he disappears. The pictures seem to close in on me, like an ache that will not go away.

10

'What did you do to him anyway?' My brother insists as we cross the street. There is a red Honda parked in front of Vinnie's house, probably Max's. It has been there all week.

'It is none of your concern,' I snap.

'Couldn't you wait until the summer to have this fight? Now we have to walk three blocks to school. You walk by his house every morning. And he's gone every morning. If you want to run into him, why don't you get here earlier?'

Because I want to torture myself. 'Bennie, shut up.'

Bennie's school is a block away from mine; I walk the remainder of the way alone, free to think. Still can't get used to it — walking alone. Once near the school I search the parking lot for his truck. It has been five days, no truck, no Vinnie. Rumours have circled around school. He is sick. He got expelled. I am worried.

Francine ignores me in class, probably uncomfortable about the whole thing as I am. At lunch-time I find myself sitting next to her.

'Hi.' Her smile is nervous.

'How are you?'

'Fine.' She stares at her food, accidentally drops her fork. I pick it up. She takes it from me. 'Perri, I hope nothing has changed between us. We're still friends?'

'Of course.' I answer, knowing it's a lie.

'Vinnie is different from any guy I've known.'

'He's special, Francine. Don't hurt him.' The words are out, before I could think them.

'Hurt him?' She is looking at me like I have gone crazy. 'He dumped me.'

'I don't understand.' I laugh even though it's not funny.

'You're really something you know that. I don't know who is more of a fool, you for being blind or him for loving you. If anybody hurt him, it was you.'

'You don't know anything,' I tell her.

'You are right. I don't know what happened between the two of you. Whatever it was, it must have been pretty serious. Enough to make him quit school. Oh, yeah, I've heard the rumours too, Perri. He's not sick, he didn't get kicked out. He quit.'

'He quit?'

'On Friday, I waited for him outside the Principal's office, trying to talk him out of it. He just quit. And it wasn't because of the fight or his grandfather either.'

'His grandfather?' Even as my mouth opens I want to stop echoing her words.

'Didn't you know? He passed away this weekend.'

I find myself looking for a chair. But I am already sitting down. 'No one told me.'

There is a frown on her face. Then it hits me. No one should have told me. Vinnie was my best friend. I should have known.

Vinnie's mother seems surprised to see me so early in the afternoon. She lets me in, leads me into the living room. Max is sprawled on the sofa. I guess she didn't kick him out after all. He raises his head, glances at me then reverts his attention to the T.V. set.

Mrs Andretti motions for me to sit. She looks old in the black dress she is wearing.

'I'm sorry about your father, Mrs Andretti.'

'He lived a good life. Died in his sleep.'

'I would have come to the funeral if I had known sooner.' I continue then choose my next words carefully: 'I don't know if you've been aware but Vinnie hasn't been in school all week.'

'I expected that. He hasn't been home since Saturday. Then again he never sleeps at home. He didn't even come to the funeral.'

'A kid with an attitude,' Max grunts.

'He was a good baby. Never had any problems with him. Now he is nothing but trouble.'

She pats my knee. 'Let me get you something to drink.'

'I'm fine, thank you.'

'Get me another one will you.' Max raises his half empty beer bottle.

'You're better looking than I remember,' he says as soon as she is gone.

I avoid his eyes.

'Gotta hand it to the kid, though, he knows how to pick 'em.'

His body shifts on the sofa. I sit away from him.

'So you're the girl who did all these paintings. His eyes circle the room and rest of the three paints on the left wall, earlier work. One is a mountain scene, the second a garden, and the third, a dark shadow walking through a park. It was as if I were seeing them for the first time. Has it been that long since Vinnie asked me over?

'You're good.'

'Thank you.'

Mrs Andretti is back. I get up. 'You're not leaving?' She says, giving Max the bottle.

'I should go. If you see Vinnie....' I stumble, unsure of what to say, 'tell him....'

A door bangs, cuts my sentence. Footsteps approach us. Vinnie enters the room, filling it with his presence. There is a hardness in his face that was not there before.

'What are you doing here?' he shoots at me.

'I came to pay my respect. I was worried about you,' I'm suddenly afraid of him.

'I'm here, aren't I?' He brushes past me. Max grabs his arm, stops him.

'Where do you think you're going?'

'I've come to get my things.'

'You think this is a hotel?'

'Let go of me. You don't own me.'

They stare at each other. Vinnie's fists clench, his knuckles whiten. 'Don't do it, Vinnie,' my lips move silently. Max releases him. Vinnie shoves past him, goes to his room. He reappears, his face white.

'Where is my stuff?'

'I packed everything.' Mrs Andretti throws a nervous glance at Max. 'We didn't think you would be back.'

'You didn't want me back. Just like you didn't want grandpa.'

'That's not true.' Mrs Andretti starts to cry. 'I couldn't take care of him.'

'He was an old man. All he wanted was company.'

'What about me? I have a life too? I need someone to take care of me too.'

Vinnie stabs his hand at Max. 'And that's what you come up with? 'You think he is going to marry you? How many of them promised you that?' His hand is like a knife in her face. 'Nobody wants you. My father didn't want you.'

My body reels back at the sound of hand striking cheek.

'How dare you talk to me like that. I was sixteen years old.'

'Yeah.' Vinnie's laugh is harsh, his hand touches the mark on his face. 'A bad time for me to come along. Screwed everything up. But you couldn't get rid of me because Grandpa wouldn't let you.'

'You don't know what you are saying.'

'That story about you being divorced, my father living out West. Bull! You can't even re- member him, can you? That's why I never found pictures. I knew. All along I knew. What was it she called me, Max? A mistake.' He grabs Max by the shoulders. 'Isn't that what she told you?'

Max remains impassive, his face blank.

Vinnie's body twitches. His eyes swallow me, blue, grey — shame. I wish I could hear the rage inside him. For the first time in his life, he is turning it within.

'Vinnie.' I move to touch him. He grabs me, raises his hand. I gasp, raise my hands to pro- tect my face. His face turns from hate to horror. He pushes me away from him. I run after him, only able to run a few blocks before I lose him.

There is nothing for me to do but go home. But that seems too easy. The track is empty at this hour. Someone has broken one of the lamp-posts. I remove my shoes, start to run, anything to quell the fear inside me. The wind pulls back my hair, plays with the folds of my dress. I tire, climb the bleachers, lie on the hard wood, not so afraid anymore. I close my eyes. Don't know for how long.

It is some time before the park lights go on. It is late and cold. A hand touches me. I sit up.

He takes my hand.

'I never wanted to hurt you.' He is trying not to cry.

'Why didn't you tell me, Vinnie? I thought we were friends.'

'Me and you, we're different but the same.'

'What do you mean?'

'I hate the truth, so I laugh at it. But you, instead, shut it out.'

'Why do you say things like that?' Does he know those words pull me apart?

'You only look at what you want to see.'

I hide my face against him. Why does it frighten me to be this close?

'I love you, Perri.'

'No.'

'I know you love me too.'

'Why do you have to change things?'

'I love you, Perri. I can't pretend that I don't. I can't go back to the way things were. You've outgrown me and it's ripping me apart. The only thing I care about in this world is me and you.' His hands cup my face. I have never felt smaller, so fragile.

'Please, Perri. Come with me.'

'Where?'

'Anywhere.'

'I can't.' I get up, needing to get away from him. He follows me across the grass, down the steps. His hands are like manacles around my wrists.

'What is so important to you here that you can't walk away from it?'

'I don't want to run, Vinnie. I have a family, responsibilities.'

'You think your father cares about you? All he cares about is that bottle he sleeps with every night. He doesn't know how to take care of you. He can't even take care of himself.'

'How can you say that? That's my father you're talking about. He's a hell of a lot better than your mother.'

His breath sucks in. I turn my back to him, so I won't have to see the hurt on his face nor let him see mine.

'You're right, at least you're useful. You cook, clean, make up great excuses for him when he is too drunk to go to work. You look after him and Bennie. You make a great mother and a great wife.'

'I hate you.' I strike at him because I know that what he is saying is true.

'No you don't. You know what you hate? You hate it that you're mother is dead. You hate it that your father drinks. You hate it that your sister left home. You hate having to take care of everybody. You hate being smart because it means people expect more of you. You hate it that things don't come easy to you.

Maybe a part of you even hates me because I tell it like it is. Just like a part of you hates your art. You know why? You paint what your eyes don't want to see. You paint with your heart.'

'Why do you want to hurt me? Why can't you leave things the way they are?'

'We always hurt the ones we love. Nothing is forever. I miss the old Perri. I don't want to let go.' The nakedness in his face shames me.

'I can't choose. Don't make me,' I beg.

He grabs me, holds me. 'It's our last summer, Perri.'

'Don't go.' I cling to him, the warmth, the nearness. I am going to lose myself, as if I'm drowning in an ocean.

'I have to.'

'Why?'

'There is nothing for me here.' His voice breaks, my heart tightens. 'Not anymore.'

I hate him. Hate him for making me feel so vulnerable, for this new ache inside me. Didn't know his mouth could be so soft, so gentle. I feel the love and anger on his lips and then a cold wind — he is gone.

My legs stumble over the steps. I see his truck. The window is locked. My fists feel numb as I pound against it. He will not let me in. 'I love you!'

He will not look at me, will not hear me. He turns. His eyes drain me.

How will I find him?

11

It is as though I am outside of myself, see myself passing his house every morning. The *For Sale* sign in the window, like a seal of approval, makes everything that happened this last month final.

This morning Mrs Andretti was at the window. She waved, looking like she wanted to ask me something. She came outside, had a bag in her hands. 'I didn't want to throw them,' she explained. You could tell she was uncomfortable. I glance at the paintings in the bag, say 'Thank you' and leave.

In school, the corridors seemed empty, the classes long. Francine has been avoiding me. Her face often mirrors my guilt. It is just as well.

'Piera?'

The sound of my name pulls me back. I stare at my plate, then at my father, sitting across the table from me. A smile plays on his lips as he eats his dinner. Has it been that long since I have seen him this happy?

'You've become a real cook, Piera. As good as your mother.'

'Everything tastes good when you're hungry.'

My brother takes the extra plate I have put to the side of the table. The one I used to set aside for Vinnie. Old habits are hard to break.

'Chew your food once in a while. You would think you haven't eaten in days,' I snap at my brother.

'I'm a growing kid,' he throws back.

'A growing pain in the ass.'

There is a bitter taste in my mouth as I finish the rest of my dinner.

My father places his hand over mine, a softness crosses his face. 'I know you miss him.'

'Hey, Papa.' Bennie shakes my father's arm. 'So what's the surprise you've been promising us?'

'It's in the garage.'

Bennie jumps from the table, I follow him into the outer room. The door is ajar. I can sense my father's excitement as he stands behind me. The light comes on. There is a red Chevy in the empty place where the Pontiac used to be. We had sold it to help pay the second mortgage on the house.

'What do you say?' My father's eyes are wide. He looks like a little boy.

'Papa... wow!' Bennie pounds him on the back. 'Way to go!'

'Piera, you're not saying anything? You don't like it?'

'Where did you get the money?'

'Your Mamma had some money.'

'Ma wouldn't have wanted this.'

My father's face clouds, his voice rises: 'I am your father. You think I'm cheating you. I know your mother saved that money for when you kids got married. You think I used it all?'

'No. It's not what I mean.'

'I did it for you.' He places one hand on my shoulder, the other on Bennie's. 'You can drive yourself and your brother to school.'

'We don't need a car. We need a house we can keep.'

'Don't worry about the house.'

'You always say that.' I shake his hand away. 'I do worry, Papa. You're not getting any younger.'

My father shakes his head at me. 'Just like your mother.'

'What a rotten egg.' My brother punches my arm. 'Come on, Papa. Let's go for a spin.'

Bennie climbs into the car, my father follows. He looks at me through the window. There is a sadness on his face. I head back to the kitchen, don't bother to clean up the mess, go to my room. I stare at the painting I finished last night. A scruffy running shoe left behind on a bleacher. The heaviness that has subtly settled inside me over the last couple of weeks presses deeper.

12

My homeroom teacher hands me a note. It is from Mr Jennings. He wants to see me in his office. I am not surprised at the request. One of my teachers must have complained about my participation in class.

'You've had word from Canadian Pacific?' Mr Jennings asks as I close the door behind me and lower myself into the usual chair.

'I received the acceptance letter last week,' I tell him.

'I knew they would be impressed by the records I faxed them.' He smiles, lazily placing his hands behind his neck.

'I really appreciate what you have done, Sir.'

'John F. Kennedy High School is proud to breed students like you. Have you thought about what you will say at the graduation ceremony?'

'No.' I pause, trying to word the decision that has been plaguing me the last couple of days. 'I've decided not to go.'

'Why?' The confusion that marks his face makes what I have to say all that much more difficult. 'Your classmates will be there,' he continues.

Vinnie will not be there.

'I have nothing prepared. I have nothing to say,' I reply instead.

'Perri, you have always been a mature and reasonable young lady. Every year I see kids walk out of this school, some with a future, and others headed nowhere. You have real potential, Piera. You are bright and ambitious. There is a whole world out there. You can make a difference.'

His well-rehearsed words make me smile.

He leans forward, as if to say something, then sits back. 'If there is anything troubling you, I would be more than happy to discuss it with you.'

'Everything is fine.'

I start to get up, eager to get away from him and the stifling room. He stops me.

'It's a shame about what happened to Vinnie. I know you two were good friends. Vinnie made a choice. He quit. Don't make his mistake. Do you understand what I am trying to tell you, Piera?'

I nod, but I am not all that sure.

'Don't throw it all away.'

The pounding of my heart is as loud as the one in my head.

Throw it away? Doesn't he know how hard I try to hold on to what I have...?

13

The door to my father's room is closed this morning, unusual since he always leaves it open. I find my brother in the kitchen mixing a pancake batter.

'Since when did you become a chef?' I ask him.

He does not answer.

'I got in late last night. Both you and Pa were already in bed, so I never got to ask you how your meeting with the teacher went.'

The kitchen is silent. I feel his body twitch next to me.

'Hey.' I put out my hand to steady him. The fork in his hand clatters to the floor. He flings himself in my arms.

'Bennie, what's wrong?'

I draw his face away from my stomach. My body turns to liquid at the sight of the bruise covering his left cheek.

'Where did you get that?'

'Don't... say... no..thi..ng, Perri. He di..d..n't... mean it,' his words come out in gulps. 'It was... my... fault. I should.. n't have... said... what I did.'

'Slowly, Bennie. What happened?'

I wait for his sobs to subside. 'I watched how much he drank like you told me. He must have been drinking since morning, because by the time we got in the car he wasn't making sense. I told him he could see the teacher another time. But he wouldn't listen.'

'Easy, Bennie.' I try to calm him.

'He couldn't understand everything my teacher said. She got mad at him because he was drunk. He started yelling at her. She threatened to report him. He got all excited, started calling her names. He was making so much noise that the security guard had to take him outside. Then I got mad at him... I told him....'

'You told him...?'

'I told him... I told him he should have died, not Ma.'

'Bennie.'

I pull him against me. Had he kept all that in? Was it so strange that he should miss her as much as I do? He was just a kid.

He looks up at me, his face pinched. 'Why does he drink so much?'

'I don't know, Bennie. Papa isn't very happy.'

'We don't give him trouble.'

'No, we don't.'

'Ma wasn't happy either, was she?'

'No.'

'Maybe if he didn't drink she wouldn't have

been so unhappy. Maybe she wouldn't have gotten sick and died.'

'Ma was sick, Bennie. She was going to die anyway.'

'Your brother is right.' The voice bursts in on us like a balloon filled with water. My father is standing before us, wearing yesterday's shirt and signs of a sleepless night. We must have woken him up.

'I should have been the first to go.' He brings his hands to his head, rubs his temples. 'She left me alone. What do I know about raising kids.'

My hands grip the chair so he will not see me tremble. I mustn't lose control. 'I have an exam this morning but I'll be back in the afternoon.'

'I'll drive Bennie to school,' he says, rubbing his chest.

How could he stand there, acting as if nothing happened? 'He's coming with me.' I say.

'I said I'll take him to school.' A red flush rises from his neck.

'It's okay.' Bennie puts his hand on my arm. 'Papa, will drive me.'

'I'm late.' I gather my books from the couch. When I get to the front door, I remember: 'You better call Mr. Tucci.'

My father does not answer; he avoids my eyes. Deep down I knew it along.

'You got fired, didn't you?'

He doesn't answer.

An invisible weight presses on my shoulders. I need to get out of here... I think I hate him.

The words on the page look like squiggles. The question marks become dots. I check the clock above the blackboard, no longer able to write. Another hour to go. Someone knocks at our door. It's Mr Jennings. I can feel everybody's eyes on me. It takes me a while to realize he is trying to get my attention. We step outside.

'They've been in an accident.'

'Papa? Bennie?' My skin feels like rubber beneath Mr Jenning's hands.

'They're all right.' There is a rushing sound in my head, like I have fallen in water. I rest myself against the wall.

'Your sister contacted us. They're at St. Michel Hospital.'

I should be fainting or crying. Isn't that what you are supposed to do? A numbness comes over me. I move, unsure of where to go.

Mr Jenning's takes my arm: 'I'll drive you there.'

We are both quiet in the car. I do not think Mr Jenning's quite knows what to say. Twenty minutes have elapsed. We pull into the hospital parking lot. We take the elevator to the tenth floor.

I can see my sister standing near my father's bed from outside the room. Mr Jennings is watching me closely.

'I'll be okay.'

'Are you certain?'

I nod. He squeezes my elbow. I try to steady my breathing before I enter the room. My sister looks up; she has been crying. She is holding my father's hand. His eyes are closed. I have never seen his face so serene.

'Is he going to be all right?'

'It will take more than a car to kill this man.'

'Bennie?'

'He's fine. He's with Paul.'

'What happened?'

'He lost control of the wheel, swerved into a pole.'

'When is he coming home?'

'He needs treatment for a few months.'

'But you said he was all right.'

'It's his liver, Perri.'

My father stirs, opening his eyes.

'I told them not to call you,' he mutters.

I pull a chair beside him. He glances uneasily at my sister. He squeezes her hand. She kisses it. The simple gesture stabs my heart. My father rests his eyes on my face for a few minutes, silent. 'Did you tell her?' he asks Gina.

'Tell me what?' I wait for my sister to speak.

'What Father means is that we both agree

that you and Bennie should come and live with Paul and I, at least until Father is better.'

'No.' I sit up, feeling like I have been jabbed with a hot poker. 'I'm not leaving.'

'We can't keep the house.'

'Sell the car.' I am desperate.

'It won't make a difference, Piera. Bennie could have been hurt today. And yesterday....' My father looks away. 'I never touched you kids. Never. I can't take care of you.' He does not want me to see his shame. 'I tried. I love you but I can't take care of you, anymore than I could take care of your mother. I broke her heart.'

'That's not true!' I hold him, wanting him to take back the words. 'I'll take care of you, Papa.'

My sister is crying. She puts her hand on my shoulder.

'You put him up to this.' I push her away.

'Try to understand.' She falters.

'Understand.' I laugh and it frightens me, because I do not sound like myself. 'Like I was supposed to understand why you walked out on us when Mamma got sick. You were in love with a guy you hardly knew. You moved in with him so you could be together. Bull shit. You found a way out. You were scared. Just like the rest of us. She was dying. She begged you to stay, but you left anyway.'

'That was a long time ago. I was young.'

'We were a family once. Then you left.

Mamma died. Now Vinnie is gone, and now you want to take Papa away from me too.'

My sister tries to hold me, but I cannot help myself. Her face is as hot as fire on my hand. She steps away from me, as though she does not recognize me anymore. The white corridors seem like tunnels as I run out of the hospital. I cannot remember if that was Mr Jenning's or not. Questions, answers, voices race through my head as I take the bus home.

The empty house frightens me. The rooms seem to get smaller. I can see my mother bent over her sewing machine. Her hair is black, like charcoal. She looks up, smiles that gentle, tired smile. I look outside the kitchen window, Bennie is throwing the ball against the wall, his face red with concentration. Gina is upstairs in her room. She holds the phone between her neck and shoulder while she paints her nails with her favourite red nail polish. Vinnie is in my room, sprawled on my bed with a book. He looks up at me, waiting to see if the answer to the question is correct. I nod, and he flashes his Garfield grin. Then I see my painting. The waves, the bodies rising above the water, trying to save each other or hold each other back. I wanted him to stay with me. What was it he said? 'Leave no threads hanging, no space empty. What are you afraid of?'

Afraid of losing what is familiar to me. I knew where I stood once, I felt safe. Then when I was not looking, it all changed. There was nothing I could have done to stop it. 'You see only what you want to see.' His words haunt me.

My father is sick. He needs help which I can't give. I can't stop him from drinking. Do I think that I can save him? How can I? I could not save my mother, could not make her live, could not make her stay. I couldn't make Vinnie stay. He knew. He understood. Nothing was forever. If I could I would paint, splash colour, fill every space, every crevice of my heart, my mind, anything to steady, hold fast, erase the terror that lived there.

I do not know how but I find myself in the cold room. In the far corner rests a painting: a sewing machine with a red-filled bottle resting on it. The broken needle drips blood. I painted it the night my mother died. I look around me. The rows of bottles all lined up on the even shelves seem to move, or is it something inside me? When the first bottle breaks and the glass shatters at my feet, something explodes inside me. A wail rises in my throat.

I cannot tell when I stop or how much time has passed before my sister finds me sitting on the cold floor surrounded by glass and drenched with wine. Her eyes shift from the floor to me.

'You made a hell of a mess.'

'I'm pathetic.' I blow my nose on my shirt, start laughing, crying. My sister puts her arms around me, rocks me like a child.

'God, that feels good.' I wipe my nose on my arm.

'I'm sorry.'

'For what?'

'For walking out on you all those years ago.' She folds her legs beneath her, sits down next to me.

'You'll get wet.'

'I'll tell you a secret, Perri. Sometimes you have to screw up if you want to learn anything. The only person I cared about was myself.'

'If you're looking for sympathy, you've come to the wrong place.' I sniff. 'You picked a hell of a time to leave. I was thirteen with a thousand questions, and no one to ask. Mamma was kind of behind with things. At least there was Vinnie.'

'You always said he had an answer for everything.'

'There are some things that you just can't tell a guy.'

'For a thirteen-year-old, you understood a lot more than I did. You knew I couldn't face it.'

'You mean, Mamma dying.'

'Yes. You're so much like her, always in control.'

'I miss her. God, Gina. I miss Vinnie. Why do people go away?' I am crying again. My sister holds me.

14

Fall is here. Sam is sitting on the veranda of my sister's house. He looks up as the door swings shut behind me. A shy smile tugs at his lips.

'So this is where you are staying.' He gets up, wipes the back of his pants.

'Yes.' I lean against the railing.

'I dropped by your house. Hope you don't mind. I picked up your mail. Your brother gave me this address.'

I take the letters from him.

'I see you're selling the house.'

'Looks like it.'

'I'm sorry about your father.'

'It's okay. He is fine now.'

He takes my hand.

'I'm sorry things ended up the way they did.'

'Me too.'

'You're going to Canadian Pacific?'

'Yeah,' I laugh. 'I finally got in. What about you?'

'Wasn't sure for a while, but I'm in. Got my letter two weeks ago.'

'I'm happy for you. It looks like everybody is going there.'

'Are you scared? About college, I mean?'

'I don't know, it seems like the logical step.'

'Don't you ever wonder if you'll screw up? What if we fail? What if we don't like it? How the hell do I know what I want to be. You turn sixteen and, all of a sudden, you're supposed to know what you want to do and who you want to be for the rest of you life.'

I listened to Sam and I've had a lot of time to think since that day in the wine cellar. Somehow Sam was voicing everything I had been afraid to admit even to myself. 'Guess we're all in the same boat,' he concludes.

Except we sail in different waters, and we have to do it alone I want to say. I do not know if he will understand.

'You heard from Vinnie?'

'No.'

He shuffles his feet, looks like he is about to say something else when the front door snaps open. My sister tucks out her head.

'Lunch is almost ready. Would your friend like to join us?'

'Gina, this is Sam, a friend from school.'

'There is plenty of food. We would love to have you.' I can tell my sister likes him.

'That would be nice but I can't. I start work at 2:00 p.m.' Sam apologizes.

'Next time then.'

He turns to me after she goes in. 'Can I call you sometime?'

'I'd like that.'

He toys with the collar of my blouse, then kisses my cheek.

'Take care of yourself.'

'You too.'

As I watch him get into his car, pull out of the parking lot and into the street, he turns around. I see myself mirrored in his face. I have changed. A sadness overtakes me. A part of my life was ending.

I look at the letters. There are two bills, a letter from Unemployment Insurance and one from the Metropolitan Art Academy. The latter feels like cardboard under my hands.

Dear Ms D'Angelo,

We are pleased to confirm your acceptance to our Academy for the Fall semester. Our director of Admissions was much impressed with your portfolio and would like to meet with you to discuss your area of interest. Would you be available to meet with....

My hands tremble. I am unable to finish it. It is as though Vinnie were right beside me, the Garfield grin playing on his face. As if he had just pulled round the street, gotten out of his truck and said: 'See, I told you so.' Who else could it have been? He must have sent them my paintings and all the drawings I made for him.

'Perri?' My sister calls through the door. 'What's the matter?' She comes out.

I show her the letter.

'I thought you didn't apply.'

'I didn't.'

She looks at me with tenderness. 'It was him, wasn't it?'

I cannot answer. She sees it in my face.

'He believed in you.'

15

The house looks large without the furniture in it, the windows bare without the curtains.

'You got everything?' I yell at my brother as I hang up on the phone with my father. We're living with Gina now. It's almost been a year since the accident. I cast a glance at the last of my paintings on my bedroom floor. The sewing machine, the child and the old man, the girl at the doorstep, the bleachers and the ocean — the painting I can't seem to finish.

'I got the last of the stuff,' Bennie shouts from the bottom of the stairs. I see him pick up the last box and bring it out onto the porch.

'Did you call Gina?' I ask, descend the stairs, go into the kitchen. The garden out back is overgrown. Can't remember when I stopped tending it. I join Bennie on the porch.

'I called her a half hour ago. She is going to be a few minutes late.'

'I'm going to miss this place.'

'Me too.' He wipes his face. 'Phew! It's hot. Where are you going?' He watches me jump off the porch.

'I'll be right back.'

The race track is empty as usual. I climb the bleachers, lie back on one of the seats. My mind wanders, as it often does. I think of Sam, Francine, Vinnie. Wonder what they are doing? Where will we all end up?

It is starting to get too hot to lie around like this. I sit up. My mind is playing tricks on me. I wipe my face. Thought I almost saw Vinnie there for a minute, among the trees. I get down from the bleachers, when I look again — it is him. He is wearing a white t-shirt. A tote bag is slung over his shoulder. He looks different, rugged, tanned, stronger. I want to wait for him to cross over but I found myself running-flying. I call his name. 'You came back.'

'I had to.' His breath is cool against my cheek.

I lay each hand against his face. He looks older somehow.

'I knew you would be back.'

'You can't imagine the feeling when I saw the empty house yesterday. Thank God, I called your sister,' he says.

'She drove you here?'

'She picked me up from the YMCA.'

'She told you what happened?'

'I'm sorry,' he nods.

'No, I'm glad. Things will be better now.' I hold him at arms length. 'Let me look at you. You're not skinny anymore.'

'I put on a couple of pounds.' He rubs his arms, embarrassed.

'They suit you. Did you make it to British Columbia?'

'No. It wouldn't have been fun without you. Besides, it's not important anymore. I ended up in Alberta, worked a couple of months in a lumber company. Made good money.'

'What will you do now?'

'I've joined the armed forces. I can make some money, plan to go back to school. Maybe take up professional photography.'

'You take beautiful pictures.'

'I was going to mail them to you but I figured I might as well hand deliver them myself. So. What about you? How is school?' he continues.

'My teachers like my work. They think its subliminal.'

'What's that?'

'I guess what they mean is that you have to look twice to actually get the picture.'

'You got accepted.' The Garfield grin is back.

'You should have told me.'

'You would have stopped me.'

'You knew all along they would take me, didn't you?'

'I'm no art critic, but your paintings, they get me in the gut.'

'You always had a way with words,' I laugh.

'You believed in me. Even when I couldn't.' I pause.

'How long will you stay.'

'Three weeks. I'll be training up in Quebec.'

'Guess it will be goodbye again. I'm leaving in a couple of weeks. I'm going to study in France this Fall.'

'That's great! Why that face?'

'It's scary, Vinnie. I'll be on my own there.'

'I'm scared too. Don't know where I will end up. Guess I knew I couldn't follow you forever. Sometimes you have to take chances. Even if it might mean losing something along the way.' His face is soft, he tugs my hair.

'Come on, your sister has one mean supper and a foot and a half devil dying to meet me.

We head back, arms around each other like old times.

'I have to lock up.' I tell him as we near the house.

I walk up the porch, make sure the door is locked, then bend take the last of the boxes. I lift the box with the carefully stacked paintings. The painting of the ocean rests beneath my chin because it is too big for the box. I study it. The moving water, the shapes that seem to cling and struggle at the same time.

We are both still holding on to each other even while we're growing apart. Walking around with the best part of each other. Vinnie Andretti and Perri D'Angelo, best friends.

Yes, it is finished, even as I started the painting I knew it was finished. My childhood, my life in this one box.

I hurry down the steps. Vinnie is waiting for me.

Achevé d'imprimer en février 1996 chez

VEILLEUX
IMPRESSION À DEMANDE INC.

à Boucherville, Québec